T0114380

Control Your Assets

Building a Solid Financial Future

Rick B. Stanzione, RFC

Order this book online at www.trafford.com
or email orders@trafford.com

Most Trafford titles are also available at major online book retailers.

Note for Librarians: A cataloguing record for this book is available from Library
and Archives Canada at www.collectionscanada.ca/amicus/index-e.html

Printed in Victoria, BC, Canada.

ISBN: 978-1-4269-0163-8 (Soft)

*We at Trafford believe that it is the responsibility of us all, as both individuals
and corporations, to make choices that are environmentally and socially sound.
You, in turn, are supporting this responsible conduct each time you purchase a
Trafford book, or make use of our publishing services. To find out how you are
helping, please visit www.trafford.com/responsiblepublishing.html*

*Our mission is to efficiently provide the world's finest, most comprehensive
book publishing service, enabling every author to experience success.
To find out how to publish your book, your way, and have it available
worldwide, visit us online at www.trafford.com*

Trafford rev. 6/11/2009

Trafford
PUBLISHING®   www.trafford.com

North America & international
toll-free: 1 888 232 4444 (USA & Canada)
phone: 250 383 6864 ♦ fax: 250 383 6804 ♦ email: info@trafford.com

The United Kingdom & Europe
phone: +44 (0)1865 487 395 ♦ local rate: 0845 230 9601
facsimile: +44 (0)1865 481 507 ♦ email: info.uk@trafford.com

Dedication

This book is dedicated to the clients' whose touch has warmed me, and to my colleagues who have encouraged and lifted me along life's journey.

Most importantly, to my wife Robin who caught my eye the first time I saw her and has held my heart ever since. You are my dream come true and the partner who always believed in me, even when I had my doubts.

For my children Breelyn, Jazzlyn and Mykklyn, you are my inspiration and what keeps me going everyday. I am forever grateful for your love and support.

Acknowledgements

First and foremost, I would like to thank all my friends and clients who have been with me through the years. I am grateful for your continued support and for the trust you have put in me. I take that trust seriously and will always work to keep it. This book couldn't be written without you.

I must thank the staff at R & R Group Inc for their excellent work. They are the backbone of our company.

Thanks also to the Expert Institute for guiding me through the process of writing this book. Their insight and editorial recommendations have made a difficult job much easier.

Finally, I would like to give special thanks to my trusted advisors and colleagues, Ellis N. Liddell, Richard Sullenger, Mark Silverman, Rock Allen, and the late Rick Wagner. I would also like to give special thanks to Karen Arthur, Compliance Analyst and her team at Investors Capital Corporation for their valuable insights that have enhanced this book and helped me navigate through the rules and regulations governing our industry.

Table of Contents

About the Author

Rick Stanzione is the President and C.E.O of R & R Group Inc. He has been involved in financial services since 1978, and formed R & R Group, Inc in 1981.

Rick's greatest satisfaction comes from meeting people and helping them achieve their financial goals and strategies. His Company's motto is "Building Relationships to Last a Lifetime!" This motto underlines his commitment to understanding his customers' needs, strategies, and goals and providing the best possible financial services.

Rick is a gifted speaker and has addressed audiences from coast to coast in the United States and Canada. He is also actively involved in many key industry organizations.

Rick is a member of the Million Dollar Round Table and a Top of the Table performer. Forbes Magazine and Goldline Research chose him as one of the Most Dependable Wealth Managers in the Rocky Mountain Region for 2009.

Rick is an active member of the National Association of Insurance and Financial Advisors. (NAIFA) and is past President of the NAIFA Bonneville Chapter in Ogden, Utah. He is also a member of the International Association of Registered Financial Consultants (IARFC).

Rick earned his Bachelor's Degree from Edinboro State University, Edinboro, PA in 1978. He did post graduate studies at Temple University and Edinboro University.

Rick lives in Utah with his wife, Robin, and daughters, Breelyn, Jazzlyn, and Mykklyn. In his free time he enjoys boating and traveling.

Testimonials

"I owe a lot to Rick! He has helped a small-town guy become financially independent in a market that has seen its ups and downs."

Dave Nordquist
Ogden City Schools

"We are not 'rich' people, but Rick spends considerable time with us on a regular basis as if we were millionaires. We are very pleased with his service and concern, and we recommend him highly."

Roger Kenneth Walter, Professor Emeritus,
Weber State University
Zora L. Walter, Retired Teacher
Ogden City Schools

"Not only has Rick helped us with our financial status, he also saved us a substantial amount on our insurances, which is a bonus we are grateful for."

Frank and Gloria Landvatter

"I have known Rick Stanzione for 10 years. I highly recommend Rick for anyone who is looking at securing their financial future. He is knowledgeable, supportive and has never failed to be there when I called. I will be ready to go when I retire thanks to Rick."

Mary Courney

"This is a recommendation concerning Rick Stanzione. He is honest and forthright. We put our trust as well as our money in his hands and it exceeded past our hopes. He has gone out of his way to help."

Delores M. Merrill
Retired Media Secretary
Bonneville High School

Introduction

Hello! I am Rick Stanzione, Registered Financial Consultant (RFC), and President of R & R Group Inc. We are a financial services company that specializes in helping hardworking people manage their money and plan for retirement. I have been in this business since 1978. In that time, I have helped thousands of people take control of their assets. When I look back on my work, I can say without a doubt that my chief source of gratification is helping people.

I have spoken for many years to groups of working people who have just retired or are nearing retirement. After meeting with them and hearing their stories, I truly believe that they are the backbone of this great country. They have worked for years to give all of us the standard of living that is the envy of the world.

I want to help people maintain the lifestyle and comfort that they deserve. This book is a call to action for the millions of Americans who are entering their retirement years, or need guidance on saving for their children's education. It is also for anyone wondering how to save for their future. This book can be the start of a brighter, more confident future.

My goal is to help you take control of your assets and live your retirement years with fewer worries about money. Think of me not so much as a financial advisor, but as a financial architect. I want to help you build a safe and secure financial foundation upon which you can create the financial home of your dreams.

You owe it to yourself and to your family to have a strong financial structure in place. This book will show how to help maximize your retirement savings, reduce taxes, and be protected from potential health cost risks that could cause bankruptcy. It will help you plan for your children's education and manage your money more effectively.

For years, many of us have worked for the same company and built up large pensions. Others believe that Social Security will help to cover the cost in retirement. Unfortunately, you can no longer depend on institutions of any kind to take care of you, whether it's the US Government or corporate pension funds. You must take control of your money to ensure that it lasts as long as you do. I will show tried and true methods that have helped millions of people just like you. There is no magic here, but the key is you taking action now.

This book will provide more than just statistics and information. I will give real stories about people who have avoided overpaying taxes, managed costs of serious health problems, and enjoyed a comfortable, secure retirement.

One of the highlights of my career was becoming a member of the Million Dollar Round Table. This is the highest recognition in the insurance and financial planning industry. I value that recognition above any other because it proves I am highly successful at helping people control their assets.

I have met and helped thousands of people through the years and have heard countless stories, both good and bad. The stories included in the book impacted me and I hope they will influence you to take action and secure your financial future.

The Three Questions Everyone Needs to Ask

When it comes to taking control of your assets there are three questions that everyone must ask him or herself. Before you meet with a financial advisor you need to seriously consider the following:

1. **What are your goals?**

2. **What are your needs?**

3. **What is your strategy?**

These three questions are the foundation of your financial structure. If you don't have any answers to these questions you really can't know where to begin. And if you don't know the answers, neither will your financial advisor.

I believe if your financial advisor isn't asking these questions, you really should consider looking for another advisor!

The answers to these questions will help me to understand your situation in greater detail.

I know from experience that most of us don't give our financial situation nearly enough consideration.

Do you have children to educate? Do you want to retire early? Do you want to travel during your retirement? Are your current investments, 401k Plan, or other investments on track and keeping pace with inflation? These are just a few of the questions that must be considered when you plan for your retirement and investments.

As the saying goes, "you don't plan to fail, you fail to plan". Without a financial plan in place your future and your family's future are placed in serious jeopardy. Take the time to sit down and think about the three questions. What are your goals? What are your strategies? What are your needs? After these questions are answered you can begin to plan for your financial future with confidence.

Investing Basics

Many people who come to my seminars don't understand the basics of investing. It is understandable that not everyone spends a lot of time monitoring the financial markets, reviewing the tax laws, or is keeping up with the current economic trends. The good news is that experienced, knowledgeable professionals do these things all the time and are available to help design your financial future. As I said before – my greatest satisfaction comes from helping people. So, let's start with some basic principles of investing.

When is the best time to invest?

Most people think that the right time to invest is when everybody else is and that is usually the time when the market is rising. That is usually the time most people are talking about how well the market is doing and it gets us thinking that we had better get in on it ourselves.

Unfortunately, that is probably the worst time because you put yourself at maximum financial risk. If you're buying at the peak of the market there is only one way for it to go, and that is down.

Investing is such an emotional activity that people tend to lose sight of the basic principles of the market. If you invest in the stock market when it is at a high point you may be paying too much for your investments. It is easy to see why investing is such a stressful and nerve-wracking experience when you see the market go up and down.

That is why I always advise my clients to: "Invest with your head – not with your heart."

We are blessed with the ability to think and plan. However, we are also blessed with emotions. Sometimes those emotions can get the better of us and influence our decisions in a negative way. Emotions often play a significant role when it comes to investing. In many ways, investing is like riding an emotional rollercoaster. In fact, the term to describe this phenomenon is called "the cycle of market emotions."

You can go from extreme happiness to severe depression, depending on how the market is doing. However, the chart below shows the point of greatest emotional high is also the point of the greatest financial risk, while the lowest point is where the greatest financial opportunities lie.

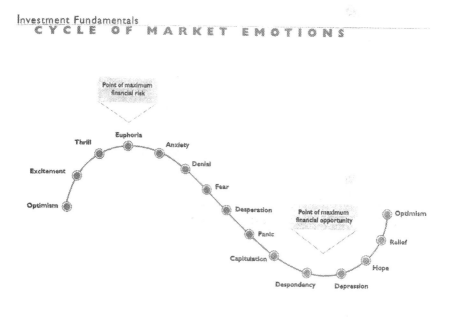

Investment Fundamentals
CYCLE OF MARKET EMOTIONS

Nor FDIC Insured   No Bank Guarantee   May Lose Value

It doesn't make sense does it? Well, that's why investing can be a challenging exercise. If we all operated like computers investing would be a lot easier, but our lives wouldn't be very exciting. My point here is that the market is going to go up and down many times throughout our lifetime and you cannot depend on emotions to make your investment

3

decisions. If the history of the markets shows us anything, it is that when you invest for the long term you usually will end up at least where you started.

So, when is the best time to invest? Based on the chart it would be at the bottom when stock prices are at their lowest. But how do you know when that has been reached? The term for gauging the perfect time to invest in the market is called 'Market Timing.' Unfortunately, without divine intervention, it is impossible to know when the market has reached that point. That is why I always tell people that the best time to invest is **now.**

When is "now?" Now is the time after you have asked yourself those three questions and have some idea of your goals, needs, and strategies? Now is when you decide to get serious about your retirement and are ready to take the next step.

How much to Invest?

"How much to invest?" This is a question that goes back to your needs, goals, and strategies. A person who is just starting out and doesn't have much income would probably need to save less than someone in their prime earning years with two college-aged children to educate.

An individual who is close to retirement and has access to a company pension plan might not need to save as much as a young father who recently started his own business. There are people who will tell you that you need to invest a certain percentage of your income. I am not one of them. I believe that every individual is different and only by getting to know your specific needs, goals, and strategies can I determine a suitable investment amount.

It is easy to tell clients that they should be saving 10 to 15 per cent of their income, or that they should be able to live on 70 to 80 per cent of their income when they retire. Unfortunately, there are no magic formulas for creating wealth unless you really know what you are trying to accomplish. And that only comes when you understand your specific needs goals and strategies.

What kind of investments do I need?

This is where the knowledge and experience of an advisor can really make a difference. Many advisors talk about balanced portfolios, but if they don't know what their client's specific goals are how can they know what they need?

When I sit down with people I want to know the answers to the three questions before I begin to think about what type of investments they need. If an older couple comes to me, I need to know if there are health issues with one of them. I need to know if one of them may require long-term care (LTC) sooner than the other. I always discuss the need for LTC because three out of every five people will use LTC if they have it. LTC also provides added protection for people because if people don't have it they risk depleting their savings at an accelerated rate. Knowing this information could be the difference between recommending an annuity, mutual fund or another suitable investment. I need to know if a client is about to retire, or not. This is an important issue and I have written a chapter on LTC to explain it in more detail.

As I will discuss later in the book, I have six plans that I believe most people should have, but I don't just hand my client a list and let them choose. I work with them to ensure that they have the right mix of investments for their specific needs. That is what controlling your assets is about.

How long do I invest?

"How long do I invest?" This question does have an answer that applies to almost everyone. There is a simple rule that most successful investors follow. When it comes to investing it is the amount of time – not the timing – that matters. Warren Buffet, arguably one of the most successful investor in the world right now put it best when he said,

"The stock market is a place where impatient investors gradually transfer their wealth to more patient investors. My favorite investment period is forever."

If anyone has had success and made money in the stock market it is Warren Buffet.

As I am writing this we are experiencing one of the most serious financial crises since the Great Depression. I wish I could tell you how it will end. Unfortunately, none of us can predict the future, but we can look back and see how the markets have responded historically.

If we look back to the Tech Bubble of 2000, when the inflated value of Internet stocks finally came down to earth, or the Market Crash of 1987 when the market lost over 3,000 points and many of us had to line up for gas for the first time in our lives. We can get an idea of how the market responds. The great thing about our free market system is that it responds to changes and puts checks and balances in place to prevent those situations from happening again. The market crash of 1987 is a good example of how the market responds because as a result of that disaster, the market now shuts down if it drops more than a set percentage in a day.

My point here is that we never know how world events will affect the market. Here are just a few of the events that have affected the markets since the year 2000.

Who Knows What Happened? 2000-2008

- **Three Extra Months of Presidential Election (2000)**
- **World Trade Center Disaster (2001)**
- **Economic Slowdown (2002)**
- **Invasion of Iraq (2003)**
- **Asian Tsunami (2004)**
- **Hurricane Katrina (2005)**
- **Market Drops 430 Points (February 2007)**
- **Oil Prices Hit $148 a Barrel (July 2008)**
- **Market Drops 771 Points (September 2008)**
- **$750 Billion Financial Bailout (October 2008)**

Those are just some of the events that affected the stock markets in the last few years. Despite all of these events, the market keeps coming back. And since I am an eternal optimist, I believe that it will come back from this crisis as well.

Since we don't know what the final results of this crisis will be, let's look at September 11, 2001. The worst attack on American soil also provides a vivid example of how risk can be managed. The disaster of 9/11 was a $94 billion insurance claim. Of course a majority of that money went to pay for loss of life, rebuilding damaged structures, restoring and relocation of businesses. But here is the interesting part; incredibly that huge sum represented only three per cent of the insurance industry's profit for that year.

How can that be? You would think that a disaster of that scale would bankrupt the insurance industry. However, the way the insurance industry works prevented that from happening.

You see, the insurance industry deals with risk by spreading it out. Many companies shared those policies in order to spread the risk. That is how the insurance industry was able to absorb one of the greatest disasters in history without collapsing. And this is the key lesson in building your retirement plan. If you can spread the risk, you too will be able to weather most financial turmoil. Let's look at some of the issues that can affect your retirement and how you can manage those risks by controlling your assets.

The Risks to Your Retirement

Wall Street Meltdown

Lehman Brothers declares bankruptcy

CitiGroup buys Merrill Lynch

An increasing number of Americans find themselves in credit card debt.

House prices falling across the country

Medical expenses rising

General Motors on the verge of bankruptcy

They are out there all around us. You see them in the news and on TV every day. These are the risks to your retirement. Hardly a day goes by without stories like those in the media. As I am writing this the American financial markets are in turmoil. Many large and powerful financial companies have disappeared and our government is implementing the largest bailout in history to save what's left of our financial system.

Many of us are concerned for our jobs, our 401k's, the value of our homes and the future.

While the headlines are shocking and the situations are uncertain, it is the information and trends behind them are posing the greatest risks to your retirement.

Did you know that 26 per cent of all Americans have decreased their retirement contributions due to rising medical costs? And that half of that number has also reduced their savings?

Believe it or not, my wife's home state of Utah was once the leader in bankruptcies in America. According to statistics from 2004, one in 35 people in Utah declared Chapter 7 or Chapter 13 bankruptcy. That was twice the national average. In 2005, the state of Utah had the third highest number of bankruptcies in America. The good news is that the state is moving down the list. In 2006 Utah was tenth and in 2007 it was twenty fifth.

A lot of this has to do with a change in the laws regarding bankruptcy but it is still a significant issue. I am sure that most of those people didn't plan to fail. No, I like to say that they failed to plan.

So let's take a closer look at the specific risks that we need to consider when we start to plan for retirement.

Longevity – The Greatest Risk to Your Retirement Savings

It is obvious that people today are living longer. We can tell just by looking around. But did you know that seniors are the fastest growing segment of the US population? This is unprecedented in our history; in fact it could be considered a longevity revolution. Let me give you some more statistics that really drive home how long we are living.

Every month one million people turn 60 years old. More than 70 million people in the world have celebrated their 80th birthday. This over-eighty group is the fastest growing age group in the world!

The average life expectancy of an American male born in 1900 was 47 years. According to the U.S. Centre for Disease Control, the life expectancy of a child born in 2006 is 78.1 years. That is an increase of over 30 years in less than a century!

The increase is even more startling for women. At the turn of the last century a woman could expect to live to about 53. Today the average life expectancy of an American woman is over 80 years of age.

But that isn't the whole story. Not only are life expectancies at birth rising, so are the life expectancies of older people.

To Age:	At Least One...
70	99.5%
75	97.2%
80	90.6%
85	75.9%
90	50.3%
95	22.1%

Source: Society of Actuaries RP-2000 Table (with full projection)

If you take a couple, both aged 65, there is a 90 per cent chance that one spouse will live to 80 years of age, and a **50 per cent chance that one in every two people at age 65 years will live to 90**. By the year 2030, the number of older Americans is expected to reach 71 million or 20 per cent of the population.

This aging of our population is unprecedented in human history and has huge social and economic consequences. It is also kind of scary.

Why are we living longer? Well, we have better health care today. We have much better medical care too. Today, we can replace body parts like knees and hips with little to minimal risk. That was unthinkable 50 years ago. We also take better care of ourselves today and have access to incredible amounts information about health care. We are better informed of the risks of certain behaviors and can choose to avoid them. All these things combined have helped us increase longevity.

Britain's Oldest Virgin Turns 105,
Edinburgh Evening Standard, October 2008.

New Zealand Woman Turns 110,
OneNews NZ, September 2003.

Columbus County Woman Turns 103
Columbus Dispatch, January 2005

How often do we see this?

Turning 100 years old is certainly a milestone today, but it is not as uncommon as it used to be.

Willard Scott of NBC's The Today Show will soon be spending over five minutes on his daily centenarian birthday announcements.

According to the 2007 U.S. Census Bureau data, there are more than 84,000 centenarians in the United States, and that number is projected to increase seven-fold, to 580,000, by 2040.

Someone who has lived over 100 years has seen incredible changes in their lifetime. Those born before cars and planes were invented have witnessed man landing on the moon. Many have witnessed the greatest victories and tragedies in human history. From World War II to the fall of Communism; from The Great Depression to 9/11; centenarians have experiences the best and worst of humanity. But what is the real impact of living over 100 years?

I know of a man who retired from professional bowling at age 106! Do you know what he said was his saddest part of his life? It wasn't putting down his bowling ball; it was losing all his friends. It is difficult to imagine for most of us, but at that age he has probably seen the majority of his friends and family pass away.

My wife's grandfather recently turned 90 years old and he and his wife just celebrated their 71st wedding anniversary. No matter where you look stories like these are becoming more and more common.

So what does that mean? It means that the greatest fear for people in the 21st Century is outliving your money. The insurance industry is now using a statistical table (2001 Commission Standard Ordinary Table) that projects insurance rates out to 120 years. The previous table only projected rates to 100 years of age.

By contrast, in the 20th Century, the biggest fear most people had when retiring was losing their money.

I grew up in an old steel mill-town, Pittsburgh, Pennsylvania, where most people retired with a fixed pension and – you guessed it – a gold watch. They weren't worried about outliving their money. Why? Because thirty years ago the life expectancy for a 65 year old was only 6.9 years or 71 and 1/2 years of age. Those people were more worried about losing their money than outliving it.

While the increase in our longevity is a positive thing, it also creates the problem of how we are going to pay for those extra years we are living.

Aging and Illness Risk

While we may be living longer, we are also succumbing to chronic diseases such as Alzheimer's and Parkinson's at an alarming rate. According to the American Association for Retired Persons (AARP), at least 80 per cent of older Americans are living with at least one chronic condition, and 50 per cent have at least two. These conditions include arthritis, high blood pressure, diabetes, dementia and cancer. There is a 25 per cent chance of developing Alzheimer's disease at age 75, and at age 85 that increases to 50 per cent. Unfortunately longevity has its drawbacks. As we get older there is a greater chance that we will require some type of long term care. According to AARP, there is 40 per cent chance that by age 65 you will be living in a nursing home.

It May Happen to you!!!

- **Age 65 – 40% chance of being in Nursing Home**

- **Age 75 – 1 in 4 will have Alzheimer's Disease**

- **Age 85 – 1 in 2 will have Alzheimer's Disease**

Source: AARP, June 2002

These are very sobering statistics. But they do make the point that we need to take control of our assets if we want to make those extra years enjoyable, and reduce the burden on our loved ones. I will speak about the issues around long-term care in more detail later in the book.

Inflation Risk

It has been said that inflation is like paying $30 for the $15 dollar haircut that cost you $5 when you still had hair.

In my mind, next to longevity, inflation is the most dangerous of all the risks to your savings. Not everyone will outlive their money, markets go up and down, but inflation rarely goes down, it usually rises steadily.

An average annual inflation rate of four per cent cuts your purchasing power in half in only 18 years. That means that just as you will need more for healthcare you will have a lot less, causing a huge drain on your savings. This is another reason why it is so important to maximize your investments.

No matter how much the necessities of life (food, shelter, and clothing) cost now, they will definitely cost you more in the future. That's the cruel beauty of inflation. Here is an example of how inflation has affected the cost of things that you buy.

The Real Rate of Inflation

Item	Cost 1970	Cost 2005	Increase
Stamp	$0.06	$0.39	5.84%
Loaf of Bread	$0.23	$2.20	7.08%
Woman's Skirt	$7.50	$55.00	6.87%
Car	$3,400	$23,000	5.96%
House	$25,600	$125;000	4.92%

As the chart shows, we are all going to face higher costs in the future and it is up to us to make sure we have enough money set aside to survive. Don't forget that as a result of our longevity, statics show for every couple who reach age 65 one or the other spouse will live to be 90. That means more of us will be paying 50 per cent more for basic necessities well into our retirement.

Fortunately, there are many simple and effective ways to beat inflation, as we shall see later.

Market Risk

As I said earlier, the stock market is a wonderful mechanism to build wealth. However, like the weather it can be unpredictable and sometimes dangerous. While in the long-term markets are an excellent way to make money, the volatility and uncertainty do provide a certain element of risk. And most of us would rather avoid risk when it comes to investing our hard earned money and saving for our retirement.

The good news about market risk is that it can be managed. While you may not be able to control the volatility of financial markets, building a balanced portfolio and spreading the risk will go a long way to helping you control your assets.

What more can I say about the volatility of the stock market? During the current credit crises we have seen incredible losses in the market. Billions of dollars of savings have been wiped out, major financial corporations have disappeared, and we are facing a financial crisis that hasn't been seen since the Great Depression. Those of you who have lived through the depression do not need to be told that investing in the stock market is not a guarantee.

However, an important part of taking control of your assets is learning to take the market changes in stride and use them to your advantage. Now, you can certainly avoid exposing yourself directly by keeping your money out of the stock market. But doing so would mean that you are losing an opportunity to grow your money faster. We all have different tolerances for risk, and as we have seen with impact of 9/11, the best way to deal with it is to spread it out.

This is where I recommend having several different types of investments. In fact, I believe that we need at least six different investment plans to sufficiently manage risk. By spreading your money in different accounts or plans, you stand a much better chance of avoiding complete financial ruin if the market collapses.

As I will discuss later in the book these plans help you manage market exposure by spreading your risk. They include a savings plan, an investment plan, a retirement plan, an insurance plan, and an education plan.

Before we start talking about managing risk, we need to discuss one more risk that we all must face.

Tax Risk

> *"The fastest way to accumulate wealth is make sure you never pay tax on income you don't use."* **John D. Rockefeller, Founder Standard Oil**

> *"The avoidance of taxes is the only intellectual pursuit that still carries any reward."*
>
> **John Maynard Keynes, British Economist**

> *"A taxpayer is someone who works for the government but doesn't take a civil service exam."* **Ronald Regan, Former President of the United States**

Mr. Rockefeller was right. And he is still right, almost 100 years later. I think it is safe to say that most of us don't like paying taxes. As Americans we have a long history of aversion to taxation. Unfortunately, to finance and manage our modern way of life, we all have to pay some taxes whether we like it or not.

One thing I am sure of is most people pay more taxes than necessary. Whether you own Certificates of Deposit (CDs), Mutual Funds, Savings Accounts, money markets, and even receive a pension or Social Security; you must remember that they all get taxed. I am not saying that you should stop paying taxes and stuff all your money in coffee cans or under the mattress.

The goal of every successful investor is to minimize or defer the amount of taxes paid on the money you earn. Sounds easy, doesn't it? Well, it can be if you have a sound investment strategy or an investment plan and use all the tools at your disposal. But as you can see, taxes can take a bite out of many investments.

Compound Annual Return 1925 -2005 After Taxes

Stocks	8.2%
Municipal Bonds	4.4%
Government Bonds	3.5%
Inflation	3.0%
Treasury Bills	2.3%

So how do you control your assets in order to minimize the effects of tax, inflation and longevity? One answer is triple compounding.

Fight the Risks with "Triple Compounding"

Triple compounding is a simple and effective method of controlling your assets and making them work for you. It is a strategy that helps your money grow faster by maximizing your savings and minimizing the amount of tax you pay on your investments.

Triple compounding refers to the combined accumulation of the interest on your principle, with the interest on your interest and interest on your tax savings. The money you would normally withdraw each year to pay taxes stays in your savings and compounds for your benefit. By sheltering as much of your savings as possible from tax you can increase your savings faster. The best way to illustrate to you the impact of triple compounding is to give you an example.

I had a client whose 80-year-old father passed away. When the family was cleaning out his belongings to give to the Salvation Army and other charities they found over $200,000 in cash stashed in the pockets of his suits, rolled up in his sock drawer and dozens of other places. I guess his dad thought the money was safe, but it wasn't working as hard as it could have. This is a great example of someone who lived through the Great Depression and still did not trust banks.

Imagine how much money he could have made if he had invested that money in a simple savings account? Now imagine if he invested it to take advantage of triple compounding. If he had invested the money in a tax-deferred savings plan, he would have accumulated interest three ways at the same time. First on the principal, second on money earned through interest and third on the money saved from taxation.

Who wouldn't want that?

Unfortunately, I hear stories like that all the time. I have heard of people who keep their money in the freezer, pin it to the inside of their curtains, stuff it in heater vents in their homes and hide it behind the carpet on a riser on their steps. Frankly, it makes me really sad that these people didn't get the proper advice on how to save their money.

This man was disciplined enough to put aside a significant amount of money, yet he didn't take that extra step and make the money grow. If you take anything away from this book, I hope it is the realization that you must take action to control your assets to ensure they work as hard for you as you did to earn them. You have to get an investment strategy that meets your needs, financial goals and strategies. And to do this right requires some assistance from a financial advisor.

A financial advisor can provide a fresh set of eyes, and see many opportunities that you can't. Also, a financial advisor who is well informed on the latest product changes can help direct your investments to earn higher returns, and protect them in a down market.

Selecting an effective financial advisor is very important and I will discuss that in more detail later in the book.

How Will You Pay for Your Retirement?

There are many risks that can prevent us from saving enough money to enjoy our retirement. Fortunately, there are even more ways to save for your retirement. Some are well established; others are a little more unorthodox. My point is that for every problem there is usually a solution. The purpose of this book is to show you as many useful solutions as possible. However, I would like to share with you one solution that I don't recommend.

On May 1, 2007, Mr. Timothy Bowers walked into a local bank in Columbus, Ohio and handed the teller a note. The teller handed him four $20 bills that Mr. Bowers then gave to the security guard and told him that today he was going to be a hero.

At first glance it would appear that Mr. Bowers was out of his mind. However, the reason he robbed the bank in the first place wasn't to get the money. He did it in order to go to prison.

You see, at the time of the "robbery" Mr. Bowers was about to turn 63 years old and had recently lost his job. Faced with the dismal prospect of minimum wage jobs with no benefits, Mr. Bowers was afraid that he wasn't going to have enough money to survive until he was eligible to receive Social Security at age 65. So he "robbed" the bank, received a three-year prison sentence, and effectively solved his financial problems in one fell swoop.

Now, some of you may think that Mr. Bowers is a fool. Others may think that he is a genius. Either way his story is certainly eye opening. Incredibly, there are people in America today so frightened about the prospect of financing their retirement that they would choose prison as a solution. By the way, his isn't the only story like this.

I do not advocate following Mr. Bowers' example. In fact, I am writing this book so that you will never have to feel so desperate about your financial future that you would consider such a solution.

Financing Your Retirement

According to a survey of Americans at, or near retirement, 70 per cent said that they had personal assets or savings that they were going to use to help support their retirement goals. 19 per cent said that the majority of their retirement income would come from their pensions and that they would use Social Security to top it up. This is where it gets interesting.

The same group of people was surveyed after they retired and the results were quite a bit different. Only 35 per cent of respondents were dependent on personal savings for the majority of their retirement income. And most of those people were afraid that they would outlive their savings.

The most disturbing result was that a whopping 42 per cent said that they were dependent on Social Security for the majority of their retirement income. Now as we all know, the Social Security system was designed to augment your retirement income not provide the majority of it. The fact that people are depending on this system for their retirement is not good.

Here's why. According to the latest statistics, there are an incredible 86 million Baby Boomers retiring in the United States. That is a huge number. The problem is that the Social Security system is already paying out $3 for every dollar it takes in. You do not need to be a math genius to realize that this is not a sustainable situation. Add to that the fact that every 11 seconds someone turns sixty in the United States, and by the year 2017 the US government will begin paying out more in Social Security benefits than it collects in payroll taxes.

How long can this go on?

I don't have the answer to that, but I believe that if something isn't done to change the system we are going to be in a very difficult situation. My personal opinion is that the first change will be increasing the age for eligibility to 70 years from the current 62. But even that will not solve the problem completely; it will only slow it down.

So what can you do? The best way to protect you and your family from the financial risks around us today is taking control or your assets. It's not as hard as you might think.

How Annuities Can Help You Save Faster and Protect your Nest Egg

In my opinion, one of the best products available for building and protecting retirement wealth is an annuity. I recommend that all of my clients seriously consider them when building their retirement savings plans. There are many opinions about annuities, but I believe that in the long run, you will pay less tax on annuities than say mutual funds.

One of the leading proponents of annuities is John Huggard, a tax lawyer in Raleigh, North Carolina. John has studied the tax advantages of variable annuities versus mutual funds and has come to the conclusion that in the long run annuities can provide a greater tax savings than mutual funds.

In fact John wrote an article called, "Fifty Reasons Why Variable Annuities May be Better Long-term Investments Than Mutual Funds", where he outlines in detail those advantages. I recommend it to anyone who wants to get more information on annuities.

While there are many advantages to owning variable annuities, I can't emphasize enough how important it is that you speak to a trusted advisor. Annuities can be complex and may not meet all of your retirement needs. Annuities are one of the oldest insurance products. They have been around for centuries and were first introduced in America before Independence.

Basically, annuities act like deposit accounts for the insurance industry. Just like you would buy a CD at a bank and get a fixed rate of interest, you can buy a fixed annuity from an insurance company and you will receive a guaranteed return. But you will also receive other benefits as well.

That is where the similarity ends. Unlike deposit accounts annuities can be modified to meet many needs. These modifications are called riders. Riders are sub-contracts that are added to your annuity contract that provide additional features, such as death benefits or guaranteed income (at an additional cost).

Today's annuity products are useful in so many ways. There are hundreds of annuity products to choose from. They can provide an income, protect your nest egg and even pay for your long-term care.

Annuities are like a map charting a course for a ship in unfamiliar waters. They provide a specific direction for your retirement or investment savings. Depending on your goals and strategies, annuities can be some or all of the following:

- **A Tax Planning tool**
- **A Income Planning tool**
- **A Capital Appreciation tool**
- **A Capital Preservation tool**
- **An Asset Protection tool**
- **A Creditor Protection tool**
- **An Estate Planning tool**
- **A Long Term Care Planning Tool**
- **A Beneficiary Planning tool**

In addition to the important functions listed above, many annuity products offer riders that provide coverage for long term care are available for purchase up to age 85, and do not require medical examinations. Other products are available up to age 90. This is very important if you are older or ill. Because as we will see, the cost of health care can be one of the greatest drains on your retirement savings.

According to Barron's a couple that retires in 2008 can expect to spend $12,000 to $15,000 a year for health care. That means that they would need to save $215,000 to cover health care costs for the first 15 years alone! If they don't, that money will most likely come out of their nest egg.

A further advantage of annuities is that they can be purchased for one spouse or both, and modified with up to date riders and other options depending on your goals and strategies.

Because annuities offer so many options they can be very complicated, and I recommend that you speak to a financial advisor when considering them.

If you want more information on how annuities work go to Appendix A, where you will find detailed descriptions of the some of the more common types of annuities (Variable, Fixed and Equity Index). There you can see which one fits your risk tolerance and meets your own goal and strategies.

Another useful feature of annuities is the option of purchasing a Lifetime Withdrawal Guarantee or LWG.

An LWG is rider on an annuity that allows minimum withdrawals from the invested amount without having to cash in the investment. The amount that can be withdrawn is based on a percentage of the total amount invested in the annuity*. (*Based on the claims paying ability of the issuer).

If used with a variable annuity, an LWG also allows you to invest in a diversified portfolio, so your assets have the opportunity to grow in a variety of market conditions. It also lets you receive an income for life, regardless of whether the markets are up or down. Even more importantly, you can arrange to have your LWG lock-in any account value gains. This is a key point because it gives you the ability to receive even higher payments for your lifetime.

An added bonus is that, like life insurance, an LWG can potentially provide for loved ones with a death benefit feature and death benefit optional rider that provides additional benefits to the beneficiary. This actually provides downside protection that 401Ks and mutual funds do not offer. Not many other investment products can do that.

I should inform you that there is a downside to annuities. Most annuity contracts require you to hold them for a set period of time. The holding period varies depending on the company and product.

If you decide to withdraw money before that time you can incur what are called surrender charges. Unlike other investments, annuity surrender charges can be very costly. This is very important to understand before you buy. Annuities function best as long-term investment products. If you are unsure about your ability to keep your annuity for the term of the contract, then annuities may not be the best choice for you.

Because of the complexity and choices of annuities, it is vital that you speak with a trusted advisor about your short-term and long-term needs and get as much information as possible before you buy.

What Retirement Planning is all about

Let me share a story from a client of mine.

My wife and I first met Rick at a seminar he presented at our retirement community. We were impressed with his presentation and took advantage of the free consultation he offered those in attendance. We had so many questions that our one consultation turned into four. Rick answered all our questions and provided us with various options that suited our estate plans and eased our tax concerns. As a result, we decided to invest our life savings with him.

Unfortunately, three weeks later, my wife suddenly passed away.

Suddenly, I needed to replace my wife's social security, pension and health benefits. Rick came to see me as soon as I called. He met with our trust attorney and my family to discuss my financial situation and come up with a solution.

Rick returned with a solution and a check for the full amount of our investment plus $2,400 in interest that had accrued in just three weeks!

Rick provided me and my family with a solution that will protect us well past the age of 100. Furthermore, he even picked up my wife's death certificate and attended her funeral.

Rick met with my family and me several more times to insure that my needs would be met with the flexibility I would need in my later years.

Through Rick, I was able to replace my wife's pension income and social security benefits. But most importantly, Rick secured the best possible health insurance plan for me at age 85!

Rick's primary concern was to meet my goals needs and strategies. He provided me with a plan that will allow my investments to last throughout my retirement.

I now have the financial security I need. Rick helped me at a difficult time and truly made a difference in my life.

Retirement planning is about more than investing and saving. It's also about enjoying your life after you decide to retire from your career or job. To fully enjoy yourself after retirement, you should have a plan on how you will spend your time and where you will live. As well, you should think about your family and how they fit into your retirement plans. Your retirement plans should go well beyond finances.

How will you spend your time once you aren't trudging off to work every day? There are lots of options for every retiree. You need to pick the one that's best suited to you and one that will keep you busy.

Vacation Forever

Maybe you want to travel, start or continue a hobby, garden, play golf, dote over the grandchildren, or even climb a mountain or two. The possibilities are endless. You've worked hard and you deserve a happy retirement. Retirement doesn't mean you should resign yourself to sitting around talking about your ailments or feeding the pigeons in the park. It should mean freedom to enjoy life and all it has to offer.

Back to Work

Maybe you will be bored with the idea of not going to work every day. If this is the case, you might be happier working or volunteering once you retire. There are lots of retirees who have started a second or even a third career after retirement. I'm sure there are many ways you can volunteer if you don't like the idea of working for money.

Health Means Happiness

What about your health once you retire? Just because medical technology has advanced doesn't mean you don't need to take care of your self. Stop smoking, watch your weight, start an exercise and nutrition program so you will be as healthy as possible in your older years. Make a commitment to become a healthier, more active person and you will reap the benefits now and later. Been putting off medical check-ups? Now is the time to get these done. Taking care of your health in your early years might help with securing health insurance at a reasonable rate once you are older.

Friends and Family

Another area that you might need to develop is friends and family. A career sometimes doesn't leave much time for cultivating friendships or enjoying your family. Once you retire, you will have more time to spend with these people but will they be there for you when that time comes? Try to make time for family and friends, even if it's just a few hours a week. The older you get, the harder it is to find and make new friends. If you ignore your family, they might not be there for you when you get older and feel you have more time for them.

In addition to investing and saving money for your retirement, now you need to make some additional plans. You need to plan how you might want to spend your retirement, where you might want to spend it, how to be healthy enough to enjoy it, and how to keep your family and friends around to help you enjoy it. This gives retirement planning a whole new meaning. Retirement shouldn't be considered an ending; it should just be a continuation of living.

The Six Financial Plans Everyone Needs

Now that you have seen the risks to your retirement, it is time to take action and get your financial situation in order. As I mentioned in the last chapter there are many ways to help reduce the risks, such as tax avoidance, triple compounding etc.

In order to use those risk reduction methods you first need to construct a sound financial foundation. I often tell people that you need more than one plan to make up a successful retirement portfolio. In fact, you need six. Most people figure that if they have an IRA or a pension that they are set for retirement. Well, if you believe that you are sadly mistaken. Not only are you putting your retirement in jeopardy, you are also exposing yourself and your family to unnecessary financial risks. Let's look at the six plans that I believe everyone should have in order to help safeguard your retirement.

1. **A Retirement Plan with Long Term Care**

2. **An Investment Plan**

3. **Life Insurance Plan**

4. **An Emergency Plan**

5. **An Education Funding Plan**

6. **A Trust Plan**

I know what you are thinking, "Wait a minute, why do I need all these? I am not a millionaire." That's the point. You don't have to be extremely wealthy to benefit from these financial tools and control your assets. Each of these plans has unique features that help you build a complete retirement. You may not need all of them, but depending on your goals for retirement, you can pick and chose which ones best suite your needs. However in my experience, you will most likely need all of them at some time during your lifetime.

If your goal is to build up savings for your children's education, an education fund is the way to go. If you want to leave a legacy of assets for your loved ones, you need to establish a trust. If your goal is to minimize the financial hardship after you have died or become disabled, then you should look to insurance.

I have chosen these six plans because they cover most aspects of financial planning and empower you to control your assets.

Let's look at each of these plans individually and see why I believe that they are important for a secure financial foundation.

A Retirement Plan – "The Retire Better Plan"

When it comes to retirement plans I believe there are two things you should know.

First, everyone needs a retirement plan.

Second, not all retirement plans are equal.

I am sure that most of you have some type of a retirement plan. Maybe you worked your whole life for a company and you have a pension. Maybe you put money into a 401K plan through your employer. Or maybe you have your retirement savings in coffee cans under the floorboards of your house. As we have seen, it happens more often than you think.

Earlier I mentioned a client who found money hidden in his parents' house after they passed away. Well, that wasn't a unique case. Another client of mine found over $200,000 in cash stashed all over his father's house in drawers, clothes and of course, coffee cans. It doesn't end there. Another client had $50,000 worth of U.S. savings bonds from before World War II in a drawer in his house. Stories like this are endless; unfortunately your money is not.

Even in the worst economic times, keeping that kind of money in your home is probably more risky than most investments vehicles. There is absolutely nothing wrong with keeping some of your savings in cash, but you have to protect it. And I will show some ways to help you do that.

As you can see not all retirement plans are the same. And they don't provide you with the same level of financial security. What good is the coffee can if nobody knows where it is? How secure is your company's pension? Everyone knows about Delta Airlines. What happened to those pensions? Who controls your 401K? Ask the former employees of Enron and WorldCom. Just because you have a retirement plan doesn't mean you are safe from the financial pitfalls.

Planning for your retirement is more complicated than opening an IRA, contributing to a 401K, or belonging to a company pension plan where you work. While these are excellent beginnings, you must plan for any and all events that can and will happen after you choose to retire from work.

You may find that your company matches up to five per cent of your contributions. That means that if you are contributing 10 per cent you may consider putting that other five per cent elsewhere to diversify your retirement plan.

You spread your risk out that way and provide better protection of your retirement assets. You not only need to plan for retirement income, you must also plan for the wealth transfer of your assets upon your death. You need to decide where you will live after retirement, how you will handle tax matters, what insurances you will need and how you will pay for it, and so on.

Planning for retirement should begin as early as possible in your life. Unfortunately most people don't start as early as the wish they did. However with some careful thought, your planning process can be started at any time during your working years. The secret is to actually put together a plan no matter what your age. The sooner you start, the more time to you will have to build your investment portfolio for your retirement income. Here are a few things that you should consider when setting up a retirement plan.

The first step in retirement planning is to start putting money aside for income. Once you have your investments set up, monitor them with your broker or financial advisor. Set up tax strategies that will help protect your assets and limit your tax liabilities when you retire. As we have seen people are living much longer, and there is a good chance you might be retired for 20 to 30 years or more. When you get close to retirement age, you should start to thinking about where you would like to retire, and whether or not you plan to travel.

If you're married, plan your retirement with your spouse. Both of you should agree on the plan and work together to insure that you get mutual benefit. If you both have a career or job, both incomes need to be taken into consideration and planning should be done accordingly.

Retirement planning is crucial. Once you reach retirement age, you will probably not require as much income for living expenses, but you could be paying out huge amounts for insurance premiums or health care. The value of your estate could be quite large and you certainly don't want to have this taxed unnecessarily.

The bottom line is that you need to take control of your assets. Start thinking about your retirement and start planning now. For a detailed description of the most common types of retirement plans see Appendix B.

An Investment Plan – "The Save for What You Need Plan"

Why do you need an investment plan that is distinct from your retirement plan? Simple, an investment plan is savings that is earmarked for something other than your retirement. Having a separate investment plan will prevent you from dipping into your retirement savings to make large purchases or if you have a financial emergency. Sometimes people comingle investments with their retirement plan and if used like that the funds are not there for their retirement years.

I would define an investment plan as a portfolio of savings that you can easily access, but is completely separate from your retirement savings. This money can be invested in mutual funds, bonds, or annuities depending on how quickly you need access to your money. I generally recommend that you keep it invested for five to seven years in an investment vehicle that fits your risk tolerance, goals and strategies. This vehicle may need to have a portion of it immediately liquid and the other could be in a vehicle more suitable to your goal and strategies (i.e. annuity products, mutual funds and united investments just to name a few).

If you are saving for a large purchase such as a car or boat, or even a second home, you might want to put some savings aside for a rainy day then you need to have an investment that is not linked to your retirement savings. Believe it or not, a lot of people have them mingled together or simply dip into their retirement savings when they need money. I cannot stress enough that you should keep your investment plan separate from your retirement plan.

In my experience, when people have them together they usually lose one. If you keep them separate then you will always have one to fall back on. This is crucial if you ever suffer a loss in your primary source of retirement income.

Furthermore, if you borrow from your retirement savings you reduce the amount of money that is working for you, and are required to pay back all or part of it depending on the product. With a separate investment plan you can avoid those problems and maximize your retirement savings.

I had a client who was a pilot for a major U.S. Airline. He had recently made a significant amount of money on an employee stock purchase plan. When he spoke to me I advised him to take his 401k (employee stock) and set up a separate investment savings plan. He could roll it over into an IRA so he would have better control of his retirement funds. Unfortunately, he didn't take my advice and lost most of his retirement savings when the airline went bankrupt. His story is far too common.

Depending on your goals, needs and strategies, your investment plan can include stocks, mutual funds, CDs and/or simply savings in an account. However you want to manage the money is fine as long as you keep it separate from your retirement savings. The good news is that when you do retire the money you have in your investment plan can be used as another source of income.

A Life Insurance Plan – "The Protect Your Lifestyle Plan"

Everyone has an opinion about life insurance. Many people don't like it. I am sure that most of you reading this have life insurance of some sort. You may have it through your employer or on your own, with reduced amounts.

I believe that life insurance is a crucial part of any successful financial plan. Why? Simple, because life insurance is designed to protect your family should the breadwinner pass on prematurely. In addition, it provides immediate cash to your family upon your death. So you not only get immediate cash payment, but you can also have income replacement as well. The other common reason is to create an immediate pool of funds available to pay off debts.

Let me give you an example. If a spouse earning $50,000 were insured for $500,000 his or her family would be able to continue living comfortably if that person dies. By taking that $500,000 and investing it **carefully** the family could continue to live off the interest alone in most cases.

It's not so much a question of "do you need life insurance?" as "what can you and your family do with it".

Insurance isn't just for protecting individuals it is also designed to protect businesses. Insurance can provide security for your business by replacing the investment of a partner or the income of a key employee.

Here is an example of how business insurance could have helped.

I know of two brothers who were in business together. They got along great. Unfortunately, their wives didn't. Realizing that there may be a problem with succession, the brothers put together a buy – sale agreement, but one of them died suddenly and the agreement was never signed.

As a result the deceased brother's wife took over his share of the company. She didn't necessarily want to, but he didn't have insurance, so she became a partner in the firm. Well, as I said the wives didn't get along, and the widow really didn't like the surviving brother. In fact she made his life a living hell according to the surviving brother. He summed up the situation this way. "If I knew it would be this bad, I would have jumped in the grave with my brother."

Sadly, his anguish could have been avoided had the business been properly insured. If the company had a policy to cover the investments of the partners, he would never have had to suffer at the hands of his sister-in-law.

The other important part of life insurance is annuities. Many life insurance policy proceeds go into an annuity. As I said earlier, an annuity is a contract between you (the purchaser or owner) and an insurance company. In its simplest form, you pay money to an annuity issuer, and the issuer then pays the principal and earnings back to you or to a named beneficiary. Annuities are generally used to provide income in retirement.

The biggest advantage of a qualified annuity is that your money grows tax-deferred until you withdraw it. The tradeoff is that if you take your money out before age 59½, you will usually have to pay a 10 per cent early withdrawal penalty to the IRS.

For non-qualified accounts there is no early withdrawal penalty from the IRS. However, there could be a penalty from the annuity company, in the form of a surrender charge. Surrender charges can vary depending on the company or the type of annuity product.

Most annuities require a holding period to avoid surrender charges. However there are many who have a zero percent surrender charge. The goal and strategies you have will determine the type that is best suited for you. The length of the holding periods can vary from zero to seven or even nine years. There are some that have 16-year holding periods. So if you are selecting an annuity you need to make sure the annuity you choose is right for your needs and investment goals.

Mutual funds and other investment vehicles may be even more risky as many of them provide no down side protection. Remember it is very important to explore your goals and strategies with a qualified advisor.

Most life insurance companies sell annuities. You pay the insurance company a sum of money, either all at once or incrementally. The type of annuity you own determines whether your money earns a fixed amount or an amount that depends on the equities in which the annuity is invested. At a designated time chosen by you, known as the maturity date, the insurance company generally begins to send you regular distributions from the annuity's account. Or, you may be able to withdraw the money over time or in one lump sum. Again you must choose what will work best to meet your goals

If you consider that one of the things in life that we are sure of is uncertainty, I don't know why anyone would refuse to protect their loved ones by not buying insurance, especially in uncertain times such as these.

An Emergency Plan – "Money when you need it Plan"

Money Market accounts are a great way to put away money on a regular basis to be used at a later date. The most common reasons I advise my clients to have one is to provide money for taxes and homeowners insurance.

A Money Market account is a type of savings account offered by banks, credit unions and some investment companies just like regular savings accounts. The difference is that these accounts usually pay higher interest, have higher minimum balance requirements (sometimes $1000-$2500), and only allow three to six withdrawals per month. Another difference is that, similar to a checking account, many Money Market accounts will let you write up to three checks each month.

If you purchase a Money Market account through a bank or credit union, the money is insured by the Federal Deposit Insurance Corporation (FDIC), which means that even if the bank or credit union goes out of business you get your money back up to a limit of $100,000, and as I write it may be increased to $250,000. However, it is important to remember that Money Market accounts offered through investment companies are **not** insured by FDIC, and can lose value due to fluctuations in the markets. This is important to keep in mind when deciding on where to purchase your money market account. I recommend that you discuss this with your advisor before choosing a Money Market account.

I include Money Market accounts because most of us are already disciplined to put money away at the end of the month. Adding another payment (this one to yourself) is relatively painless for most working people and much safer than pinning it to the back or your drapes or putting it in the icebox. You can also use Money Market accounts to deposit any lump-sum payments you may receive, such as tax returns, legal settlements or lottery winnings prior to investing them. Money Market accounts are safe harbors for your funds, but I don't recommend them as an investment because they won't keep up with inflation and are usually designed for short-term investments of less than a year.

An Educational Funding Plan – "The College Fund"

Putting money away for your children or grandchildren's education is vital. The cost of higher education is rising at an alarming rate and if you want to give your children the opportunity to go to college you will need to have money set aside.

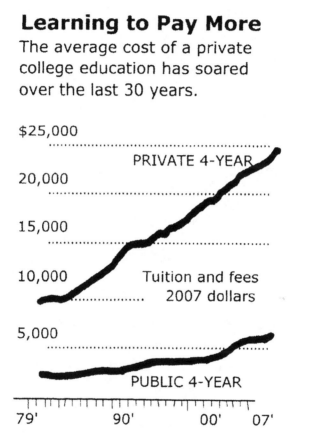

Learning to Pay More
The average cost of a private college education has soared over the last 30 years.

There are two primary types of savings plans that allow you to save money for your children or grandchildren's education. They are the Uniform Gifts to Minor Account or UGMA and the 529 Plan.

I recommended that a 529 Plan should be part of your financial portfolio because depending on the plan; you can use the savings for yourself if it is not used for educational purposes. They both provide tax-deductable savings; however there is a big difference in how the money can be used.

39

You should consider this difference when setting up any savings plans for your kids.

The Uniform Gift to Minors or UGMA Account

An UGMA is available in all states under various statutes or through the Uniform Transfers to Minors Act. The main benefits of the account are that the gifts are tax-free to donors and can potentially lower your overall estate and perhaps inheritance taxes. As well UGMA accounts can reduce a parent's overall tax rates. When a child or recipient reaches age 14, the earnings are usually taxed at their tax rate – which is usually lower than yours.

However, as with all savings plans there are some potential drawbacks. The Uniform Gift to Minors Act specifically provides that once money is transferred to the account, the donor cannot take it back. That means that once the child reaches a maximum age (set by each state), only the child can make withdrawals. Until that time, the account must have a custodian, which is usually the parent. If you set up an UGMA and you are also the custodian, but you die before the funds are turned over to the beneficiary, the account will be taxed as part of your estate.

Another important consideration is that any withdrawals or distributions from an UGMA must benefit the child. These distributions generally include college expenditures, summer camp or other activities that only benefit the child. Technically, if a custodian uses money in a manner that doesn't benefit of the child, the child could sue to recover for misappropriation of their UGMA.

Why a UGMA isn't for everyone

Believe it or not, students who are eligible for financial aid may actually not benefit from having a UGMA. Colleges and financial scholarships generally assume that 35 per cent of assets in a child's name be used to pay tuition before calculating any award of financial need. This figure is approximately six per cent of parents' assets. That means that any potential tax savings could be significantly offset by the loss of financial aid given by the school. To combat this financial aid conflict, many parents sent up UGMA accounts and then plan on using the assets for the benefit of the child prior to completing financial aid forms; therefore, they receive the tax benefit and avoid losing financial aid.

So consider your options carefully before you open an UGMA Account. If you want to save money for your child and don't care what he or she does with it, then an UGMA Account is fine. However, if you want your child to use the money strictly for education then you should consider a 529 Plan.

529 Plans

A 529 Plan is a tax-advantaged savings plan designed to encourage saving for future college costs. 529 Plans are sponsored by states, state agencies, or educational institutions and are authorized by Section 529 of the Internal Revenue Code, which is where they get their name.

There are two types of 529 Plans: pre-paid tuition plans and college savings plans. All fifty states and the District of Columbia sponsor at least one type of 529 Plan.

A 529 Plan, unlike an UGMA can only be used for educational purposes. If your child or grandchild decides not to go to college that money reverts back to you. This is a significant difference and one that most parents will appreciate. If your goal is to save money for your child's education, then the 529 Plan is preferable. As every parent knows you can't control what your children do. If they don't want to go to college that's fine, at least you know your options.

With the 529 Plan you can always transfer the money to the next child or if your child is fortunate enough to earn a full scholarship, then you can take that money and invest it as you see fit. You can put it in an IRA or another secure interest-bearing tool – the choice is yours because you get to keep the money.

The most vivid example of the flexibility of the 529 Plan is an ad that ran on TV a few years ago. Perhaps you have seen it. A couple is seen at the kitchen table worrying about how to save for their daughter's education and wondering if they will have enough money to send her to college. In the next scene the same couple is seen ten years later talking about how time flies. The daughter runs in and joyfully tells them that she just earned a full scholarship to college. The parents turn to each other and say, "College Fund". In the next scene we see a large yacht pulling out of the dock with "College Fund" across the back.

A Trust Plan – "The Avoid Legal Limbo Plan"

I always encourage my clients to get a trust even though I don't sell trusts or make any money on them. I believe a trust is a very important part of your estate plan and crucial to your retirement portfolio.

What exactly is a trust? A trust is a legal arrangement under which one person, the trustee, controls property given by another person, the trust maker, for the benefit of a third person, the beneficiary. When you establish a revocable living trust, you are allowed to be the trust maker, the trustee, and the beneficiary of that trust.

Some clients ask me if a will won't do just as well, my answer is, "No."

While it's true either a will or a trust can say, "Who gets what" when you die, only a trust can also speak for you when you're mentally or physically disabled. Wills only work after you're dead. Without any written instructions in a will or a trust, your estate could be stuck in legal limbo (including probate) for years. It doesn't matter how large or small your estate is, if you do not have a valid trust, and/or will, control is out of your hands.

When you have a trust, you normally also have a will which names the trust as its only beneficiary. Trusts only control property owned by the trust or payable on death to the trust by beneficiary designation. Lawyers call this "funding your trust." If anything is left in your name when you die the 'pour-over will' puts it into the trust, but only after the court authorizes the executor of your will to do so. A lawyer I work with calls the pour-over will a "legal pooper scooper" because it will clean up after you, but you'd rather not use it because like any will it must go through probate. You won't need to use the pour-over will if your trust is fully funded, but it's good to have it just in case and you'll still need it to name guardians for your minor children.

If you decide, like me, that a trust is the way to go and you're married I'd recommend that each spouse have their own trust rather than the more typical one joint trust for both spouses together. Having two trusts, one for each spouse can help protect the assets of one spouse from the liabilities of the other. Contrary to popular belief, you're not generally liable for the debts of your spouse just because you're married unless you contractually obligate yourselves to be, or you own your property in joint name (or a joint trust), or your spouse incurs major medical expenses. And since you can name both spouses as co-trustees of each of your trusts, either one of you can access the funds in the other's trust, just like when you owned it jointly, but your creditors can't!

Avoiding legal limbo means both efficient transfer and effective receipt of your assets when you pass. Most married couples accomplish a fairly efficient transfer on death from one to the other because they own their property jointly and they name each other as beneficiaries on their life insurance policies and retirement plans like 401ks and IRAs. However, you should know that the efficiency is lost when the second spouse dies or, in the case of joint property, if they both die at the same time.

Properly understood, crafted, and fully funded trusts are quite efficient transfer tools, and can be far more effective in the protection of the wealth you pass on to your heirs. For example, if you leave your property outright to your spouse, or children, then their future creditors can get at it. This means that if your heirs are involved in lawsuits (tort or contract), divorce (in-laws becoming "outlaws"), bankruptcy, or government spend down to qualify for benefits (such as Medicaid) their inheritance is at risk.

For the sake of your loved ones, I recommend you trade a less efficient wealth transfer tool for a much more effective and protected one.

Even the State of Utah must recognize the value of these protective trusts. Otherwise why would they have changed the law governing trusts in 2004 to allow them to last for 1,000 years?

While trusts are designed to handle your property, you also need be aware of the new Utah Advance Health Directive (UAHD). The UAHD allows you to authorize someone to make decisions concerning your medical care on your behalf when you are no longer able. This is especially important for your loved ones who may be burdened with the difficult decision of when to stop medical intervention and allow natural death.

A good example is my uncle. He was a fit 60-year-old man who exercised daily and had no serious health issues. Unfortunately, one day while he was stretching before a run he had a massive heart attack followed by a stroke that rendered him brain dead. My aunt was convinced he would recover. She initially refused to believe that he would never regain consciousness. Sadly, he didn't have any advance medical directive, so she was forced to make the heart-wrenching decision to end her husband's life. Just imagine the anguish that could have been avoided if my uncle had prepared a trust and included a do not resuscitate (DNR) directive?

The most famous example of an estate that didn't have a trust is John Wayne. That's right; The Duke didn't have a trust. In fact, he didn't even have a will when he died. As a result, his family fought for years to settle his estate. Imagine how much money, time and stress his family would have been spared had John Wayne prepared a will and a trust. For that reason, I recommend trusts as an invaluable part of your portfolio.

When you set up a living trust, you transfer ownership of all the assets you'd like to place in the trust from yourself to the trust. Legally, you no longer own any of the assets in your trust. Your trust now owns your assets. But, as the trustee, you maintain complete control. You can buy or sell as you see fit. You can even give assets away.

Upon your death, assuming that you have transferred all your assets to the revocable trust, there isn't anything to probate because the assets are held in the trust. Therefore, properly established living trusts allow you to completely avoid probate. If you use a living trust, your estate will be available to your heirs upon your death, without any of the delays or expensive court proceedings that accompany the probate process.

One of the myths about trusts is that since they avoid probate there's nothing to do when you or your spouse dies. Actually, that is not the case. There is work to be done to ensure the trust is fully implemented at your death and an attorney can help. However, I recommend that you arrange this with your attorney now so that you are better able to negotiate the details such as what services they will provide and how much it will cost.

There are some trust strategies that serve very specific estate needs. One of the most widely used estate tax avoidance tools is a living trust with what's often called an "A-B" provision. I've found that throwing acronyms around can actually confuse clients so let me explain. I like the way one attorney I work with describes it.

Estate tax is the last tax you (or really your trustees on your behalf) will pay. The estate tax is currently a 45 per cent tax (the highest tax rate we have in the U.S.). Fortunately it has two exemptions. The first exemption allows you to leave an unlimited amount to your spouse. The second allows you to leave a limited amount (currently $2,000,000, although it's been as low as $600,000!) to a non-spouse such as your kids. That limited amount is called the applicable exclusion amount. Without getting into a lot of tax or legal mumbo jumbo, I like the way an A-B trust enables you to pass on up to double the exemption amount to your heirs free of estate taxes.

When an A-B trust is implemented, two subsequent trusts are created upon the death of the first spouse. The assets will be allocated between the survivor's trust, or "A" trust, and the decedent's trust, or "B" trust.

This will create two taxable entities, each of which will be entitled to use a personal exemption.

The surviving spouse retains full control of his or her trust. He or she can also receive income from the deceased spouse's trust and can even withdraw principal from it when necessary for health, support, or maintenance.

On the death of the second spouse, the assets of both trusts pass directly to the heirs, completely avoiding probate. If each of these trusts contains less than the exemption amount, these assets will pass to the heirs free of federal estate taxes.

Problems with Trusts

While having a trust is vital, there are problems with trusts. In fact, there are three problems that I see all the time.

The first is that people don't always know what is in their trusts. I get people coming to me with huge binders, they slam it down on the desk and say, "here is my trust". Well, I suggest that you take the time to review your trust so that you know what is in it. If you find that it is too difficult to understand, have a professional review it with you and answer any questions you may have. I do this all the time with my clients, because I know how important it is that people understand their financial situation so that they can control their assets.

The second is that people don't update their trusts. Trusts are living documents and they must change when your circumstances change. Some of the things that affect your trust are loss of spouse to either divorce or death, or the sale of property or other significant assets.

The final problem that I find with most trusts is that people do not fund trusts correctly and sometime not at all. It has been my experience that many people fail to set up accounts to handle the financial activities that are stipulated in their trusts.

These are just three of many changes that directly affect your trust. Trust laws differs from state to state. For example, in the state of Utah, the law regarding trusts has changed. As of January 1, 2008, you must have the medical directive portion of your trust updated in order for it to be considered valid. So be careful, if your trust was set up more than three years ago your state may require changes as well.

The bottom line is this; know what is in your trust and keep it updated if you want to avoid costly and time consuming probate issues. I recommend reviewing your trust at least every year but no less than every two years to make sure that changes in your life are reflected in your trust. Again tax laws change enough to warrant that annual review too.

The Truth about Long-Term Care

"We have caregivers who end up in the hospital long before their Alzheimer patients pass away." – **Gladys Zobel, Alzheimer Disease Association of Kern County.**

The greatest gift you can give to those you love is your own independence. The essential truth about long-term care is that it can be very costly if you do not plan properly. And that burden will likely fall on your loved ones. I always advise my clients that Long Term Care is not an investment for you; it is a gift of love.

I come from a big family. I am Italian on both sides, and I vividly remember how our family dealt with caring for our grandparents when they became ill and couldn't care for themselves.

When I was a kid, I remember my dad saying to me, "Rick, get your sisters and get in the car. We are going to over to your grandparent's for the week to help take care of Grandpa".

My parents, aunts, uncles and cousins all took turns looking after our grandparents. One week it would be our family, and then the next week another relative would do the same. You see my dad had five brothers and five sisters. Large families are rare these days. Family demographics are totally different today than they were 30 years ago.

Americans move around today without even thinking about it. It is not uncommon today for family members to live on different coasts or even overseas. People get transferred for work, they move looking for opportunity, or they just want to live somewhere with a better climate. With the advances in communication technology we don't need to be near people to stay in touch. We have email, cell phones, and most importantly, free long distance calling. As a result, people are more free to move than ever.

That is why the burden of caring for an elderly or ill family member increasingly falls to the closest family member. No one plans it that way, but more and more that is how it ends up.

Sooner or Later…

So, what happens to our loved ones when they need help? This is where long-term care comes in. Long-term care benefits are the best way to ensure that you don't burden your family unnecessarily. I believe that it is also the reason that fewer people are going into nursing homes.

Sooner or later we are all going to die. I hate to be the one to tell you that, but I am sure you aren't surprised. When it comes to taking control of your assets, death is one of the two certainties in life. The other as you all know is taxes. What a lot of us don't think about is what happens when we become too ill to take care of ourselves? Many of us have relatives who are reaching that point. Some of you may have been diagnosed with chronic degenerative diseases such as Parkinson's or Alzheimer's.

The reality is that as we live longer, we are more and more likely to end up requiring some sort of assisted care. In many cases we will not be able to live on our own or with our spouse. This is where long-term care benefits help protect your nest egg. Remember that if you do not have LTC protection you will have to use your saving or retirement fund to cover your health care costs. This significantly increases your risk of out-living your retirement nest egg. Without LTC coverage you are not only using your savings to take care of your additional health needs, but you are depleting your retirement nest egg at an accelerated rate.

Types of Long-Term Care

Traditionally when we think of long-term care we think of nursing homes. However, long-term care encompasses many other types of institutions and services that help people manage their day-to-day lives. In fact, the number of nursing homes in America is declining rapidly.

Long-term care includes all the different types of assistance that a person might need if they are unable to care for themselves for a prolonged period of time. People can receive long-term care at home (commonly known as home care), in an assisted living facility, or in a nursing home. Many people require some type of assistance but are not completely dependant on a caregiver. For example, assisted care living facilities allow people to live in their own apartment or condo, but have access to common eating, health and recreational areas when necessary.

Then there is in-home care, where people remain in their home or apartment, but have someone come in and help them with the daily activities necessary for living.

It is important to understand the different types of care because the costs can differ greatly. As well, knowing the differences helps you choose the correct type of investment (annuity, mutual fund, unit investment trusts, stocks, etc.) to cover these costs should you or your spouse ever need long-term care. As we saw earlier, with increased age comes increased risk of chronic illness or disability.

Determining the need for Long-Term Care

As we saw earlier, we are living longer now. But people rarely just suddenly stop functioning. So, how do you know when you or a loved one is in need of some form of long-term care? Sure some people may have a stroke or sudden fall and be left unable to care for themselves. But, for many people the progress is so gradual that they don't realize it.

That is where the Activities for Daily Living (ADL) index and Instrumental Activities for Daily Living index (IADL) come in. These are two tests used by health professionals and the insurance industry to determine if an individual is capable of caring for him or is in need of some type of long-term care. It is important to know these indexes so that you can recognize possible needs in your family.

Basic Needs

We all need to be able to do certain things to live well independently, but how do we determine who qualifies for long-term care? The Activities for Daily Living index or ADL, consists of activities that we all need to be able to do to survive.

1. **Eating**

2. **Bathing**

3. **Dressing**

4. **Continence**

5. **Mobility**

6. **Transferring**

This is a standard benchmark used to determine who is in need of help. Generally speaking a medical professional will assess an individual on his or her ability to perform these tasks.

By definition, if someone is judged unable do just **two** of those six activities he or she qualifies for some form of assisted care. How many of you have a parent or relative that is at or near that standard?

By the way, these are just the basic tasks required for living.

Living Independently

The Instrumental Activities for Daily Living, or IADL, includes activities that an individual needs to perform on a regular basis in order to live independently such as:

1. Traveling outside the home

2. Maintaining your household finances

3. Preparing meals

4. Housework or gardening

5. Using a telephone or computer

6. Taking medication properly

While they are not as basic as the ADL tasks, they certainly contribute to the quality of your life and independence. In some ways people who are able to manage the ADL tasks but have trouble with the IADL tasks are in greater danger. How many of us have a loved one who lives alone, but shouldn't? They may still manage fairly well, but it is getting harder for them. They forget to turn off the stove, misplace money or are unsteady on their feet, but insist on living independently.

As we have seen from the statistics there is a very good chance that you or someone you love will end up requiring long-term care. That is why it is important to recognize these tasks. That way we can step in and get the necessary help to maintain a decent quality of life in our retirement years.

It's Time to Take Action

Now that you have seen the risks to your retirement and the methods of managing and reducing those risks, it is time to talk about taking action.

What do I mean when I say taking action? Simple, I want you to spend some time thinking about your investments and retirement savings plan. Whether it is a company pension, a 401K, an investment portfolio or insurance and annuities, it is time to examine your situation and make some decisions. Most importantly, I want you to be able to analyze and start building your financial foundation. Eventually, this might involve the help of a financial professional, but it needs to start with you!

As we have seen, the Social Security system is not going to be able to provide you with enough income to survive comfortably. Even if you have lived modestly, Social Security alone will not keep you in the lifestyle you are accustomed to. Remember Social Security was designed to supplement one retirement income, not as a retirement plan!

Here is a question that I frequently ask my clients. Do you know what would happen to your family if you didn't wake up tomorrow? Do you have a life insurance plan that will replace the income of your spouse to take care of you and your family? Remember no one knows what your family may need better than you.

Do you know what would happen to your spouse if you became ill and couldn't work? Do you know how he or she would manage if you required constant care? If you work or are considering going back to work, do you have a long-term care (LTC) plan that will meet your needs? Not just for a three to seven year period, but for your lifetime.

Many individual plans provide a specific benefit for a specified period of time. However, once the benefit amount is exhausted the there is no more coverage. With the steep increase in health costs, it is very possible that your benefit might be used up in the first few years of the policy period, forcing you to tap into your retirement funds. That is why you must have a plan to meet your strategies.

Some insurance policies and annuities offer LTC benefits as a rider for a lifetime and not just a specific period of time.

Why am I asking these unpleasant questions? Because we all need to think about these things whether we like it or not.

I believe that most of us would hope that our families would be taken care of if something should happen to us. But we can't just rely on hope and faith. You need to take action. You need to take control of your assets and manage them in the most prudent way possible.

Throughout this book I have talked about the various methods for taking control of your assets. However, the first step is your willingness to look at your financial plan and decide to take action. As the Chinese proverb goes, "A journey of a thousand miles begins with the first step". That is how I believe you need to approach your future.

Try to have a long-term outlook. Don't get distracted by the events of the day, or the negative headlines in the media. I know this isn't easy. It requires you to focus and assure yourself that your choices are right for you. It will help if you have confidence in your financial advisors. Start with one of the six plans mentioned to establish a benchmark. Don't let it overwhelm you. There is no need to feel embarrassed about seeking professional help from a qualified financial advisor, once you know your financial goals and strategies.

How important is to you? If the answer is very important, then this exercise is worth doing to insure that you meet the goals and strategies for securing your future and your family's. If you don't do it who will?

You can only meet your goals and strategies when you start planning. If you never start, you are just like the guy who wants to win the lottery but never buys a ticket.

Evaluate your Goals, Needs and Strategies

If you don't have a map how can you tell where you are going? The same principle applies to financial planning. You must understand what you want for your financial future in order to create a plan.

Remember the three questions. What are your goals, needs and strategies? Make sure that your income stream meets your requirements (Needs). Make sure you understand your options and how well they match your risk tolerance (Strategies). Make sure the financial products are right for what you want to achieve (Goals).

Again, if this sounds overwhelming do yourself a favor and get a financial advisor who can assist you in your endeavors.

There are no shortcuts to this step I am afraid. You need to sit down and think. Think about your goals, retiring in luxury, traveling the world, or taking care of the grandchildren. Think about your needs from a financial, medical, and spiritual point of view. Take time to think of your strategies and how you will achieve them. Allow yourself some time in a quiet, uninterrupted environment with your spouse, partner or key family members. Establishing a balance may be the key to achieving your goal and strategies.

Seek Expert Financial Help

I can't stress this point enough. Financial planning can be a very confusing and complex business. There is no sense in trying to figure it out your self, when there are qualified professionals are available to help. In fact, you will probably be doing more harm than good. That is why it is in your best interest to get experienced professional help when building your financial plan.

I believe that the three most important people to your financial success are:

- **A Financial advisor,**

- **A CPA or Tax Preparer,**

- **A Trust Attorney.**

I strongly recommend that people over 50 have at least these three people helping them with their finances. As you get closer to retirement you need to pay more attention to your financial plan and it may get more complicated. Because our lives constantly change, it is important to review your plan at least on an annual basis.

Do your legwork and choose a financial advisor who has your best interest at heart. Choosing an advisor is not always easy. But there are some things you can do to protect yourself from bad advice.

The first thing that I tell my clients to do when I meet with them is check my profile on FINRA, the Financial Industry Regulatory Authority. FINRA is the organization that regulates all securities firms in the United States and sets the standards for financial advisors. It isn't part of the government, it is an industry-run organization that works to keep investors informed and help protect them from financial services fraud.

I have been registered with FINRA since it was created in 2007. Prior to that is was the National Association of Security Dealers (NASD). NASD merged with the New York Stock exchange in November of 2007 and formed FINRA.

FINRA is also a great place for you to go to get information on financial planning. They have a great website (www.finra.org) where you can get information on investments, check the credentials of your advisor, or broker dealer, and most importantly, see if there are any complaints about him or her. You can also use the site to file a complaint if you feel that you are not being treated fairly.

I also recommend that you check and see if your advisor is a member of other widely recognized industry organizations such as the Million Dollar Round Table (MDRT) or the National Association of Insurance and Financial Advisors (NAIFA). MDRT is the premier association of financial professionals worldwide, and NAIFA is the national organization representing insurance and financial advisors.

In addition, there are many other non-profit organizations that provide information. The Society of Financial Service Professionals (FSP) is one such organization. FSP has founded the Partnership for Retirement Education and Planning (PREP), where financial services professionals are encouraged to help Baby Boomers in their communities take action in preparing for their retirement.

Other organizations that provide information include, the American Council of Life Insurers (ACLI), Association for Advanced Life Underwriting (AALU), Association of Health Insurance Advisors (AHIA), GAMA International, Insurance Marketplace Standards Association (IMSA), Life and Health Insurance Foundation for Education (LIFE), National Association of Independent Life Brokerage Agencies (NAILBA), and Women in Insurance and Financial Services (WIFS). Feel free to check with these organizations to help you choose a qualified advisor. For the web addresses of these organizations go to Appendix C.

It is my experience that the more active a financial advisor is in his or her profession the more likely that he or she is really committed to making a difference in peoples' lives!

Second opinions are not a bad thing to get either. I always tell my clients who are shopping around for an advisor to come back to me with their best plan. Then I ask for a last look to insure that they really are getting the proper advice.

First I make sure that they have a customized plan that meets their needs, goal and strategies. I also look to make sure that the plan is flexible so it can be adjusted to meet emergencies and un-foreseen situations in the future. If the plan doesn't have those two elements, I advise that they go back and talk to their advisor.

While no one is perfect, I always put my clients' goals, needs, and strategies first when preparing a financial plan. When looking for an advisor make sure that he or she does so as well.

Another important thing to do when seeking professional help is asking for references. A good financial advisor should be more than happy to provide you with the names of some of his or her clients as references.

Finally the most important thing is that you find an advisor that you like and trust. If you feel comfortable with your advisor you are more likely to feel comfortable with your financial choices.

Work with your Advisor to Build a Plan.

Once you have found an advisor that you like, it is time to sit down and start building your financial plan. You should be meeting with your advisor as often, and as long as you need to feel comfortable. At minimum, you should meet with your financial advisor annually.

I spend hours with my clients going over their goals, needs and strategies to make sure that I understand what it is that they want. I believe no one can invest your funds with out knowing what your needs, goal and strategies are now and in the future.

Your advisor must be willing to put in the time to understand your situation. Remember, anyone can sell you something. You need to ask yourself whether you want a salesperson or a financial advisor.

I recently met with a client who had purchased a "second to die" policy from another agent. With a "second to die" policy both spouses must pass on in order for the beneficiaries to receive the death benefit.

My potential client told me that he and his wife had put $300,000 into this policy as a single premium. When I asked them the purpose of this policy they told me it was to give their children $1,000,000 when they died. The agent also told them that it would be tax free upon their death.

Unfortunately, by over-funding this with the lump sum they put in as their premium the policy became a "Modified Endowment Contract" and this type of policy is taxable. To make matters worse – they had a 20-year surrender charge, and if they cashed it in now (four years into the policy) they would loose $40,000. And worst of all, since he is 85 years of age, should he need to withdraw any funds from his policy for an emergency, or to pay for health care, he would also have to pay taxes on any gain on the premium basis.

This is an excellent example of an agent just making a sale and not listening to the clients' goals and strategies. The result is the client suffers.

By working with this couple, I was able to offer them a solution that limited their losses and still allowed them to provide for their children. Unfortunately, by surrendering their current policy they would have to pay $40,000, but they would not have to pay taxes on the new policy. I recommended investing the remaining funds from the surrendered policy into a seven-pay Single Premium Annuity (SPIA); we were able fund the new policy with seven separate premiums annually. This allowed them to fund the policy at the maximum yearly amount for seven years with no tax implications on any cash funds he may need to withdraw from the policy. Most importantly when they both die, their children will receive the $1,000,000 death benefit tax-free and should they need to use the cash value prior to their death, there would be no tax or penalty.

Unfortunately for this couple, these costs and concerns could have been avoided if the original agent simply reviewed their goals and strategies, and acted in their best interest.

The most important aspect of my job is to understand my client's needs. I cannot provide proper options if I don't know what is going on with them. I want to give my clients the best possible choices. To do that I need them to tell me what they want. I also need them to provide me with information.

I encourage all my clients to bring as much information to our meetings as possible. No item is too small or insignificant. I look at everything including: income statements, debts, mortgages, assets, contracts, financial statements, etc. I may not do anything with a lot of the data, but it helps me see the big picture and what you are trying to achieve. You must establish a benchmark to start the process of defining goals and objectives.

Remember, if I don't know all the details I can't provide you with the best possible solutions.

Here are just some of the documents that you should have when you meet with your financial advisor:

- **Mortgage,**
- **Mutual Funds,**
- **CD's,**
- **Money Markets accounts,**
- **Brokerage accounts,**
- **Bank statements (recent and old),**

- **Bonds,**

- **Stocks,**

- **Life & Annuity accounts.**

I cannot stress enough how important it is for me to have as much information as possible. I recently met with an 81 year-old client. After going over his information for two hours, and deciding which products would work best for him, he said, "By the way I have a stock account that is valued at $250,000." He did not want to move it because it had doubled in value since he purchased it 25 years ago.

It turns out that this account represented approximately 20 per cent of his total portfolio. It was a significant part of his financial picture and changed the way we set up his plan.

I advised him that should the market go down, how long could he wait for the market to come back if he needs these assets?

He thought about that for a few minutes and told me to move the money into safer investments where he would not have to worry about losing it.

Coincidently, he transferred the money on August 12, 2008. As you know, one month later the market crashed and he actually called to thank me. Although I have no crystal ball, and take no credit for his timing, I will take the credit for listening to his needs and goals. Because of that, I was able to offer him a few choices to help safeguard these assets, and fortunately he listened to my recommendations. I get so much gratification from helping people like this.

Remember, the more information I have the better the plan we can create. If your advisor is hesitant to spend the time with you, or says that he or she knows what you need, it's time to get another advisor.

First and foremost, financial advisors need to be good listeners. That is the best way to understand you and your goals. Only then can they offer choices that can work for you. It's a two way street "Your goal and strategies and his expertise". It has to be a win-win situation or don't waste your time!

Stick to your plan

This is much easier said than done. Life just doesn't want to make things simple for us. Things change, jobs, family, you name it. This is why I cannot stress enough how important it is that you review your accounts at minimum on an annual basis. If you need to do it more often then do it! Because your situation can change from year to year it is crucial that you stick to your plan as best you can. An annual review helps you do just that.

I am not saying that you need to go bankrupt, or let your kids go without new shoes in order to stick with a financial plan. If that means only getting a 40" plasma TV, so be it. If it means that you drive your car for a few extra years, that's fine too. You need to keep in mind that the money you are saving now is for your use in the future. It is easy for people to live for today, but an important part of taking control of your assets is also looking to the future.

I recommend an investment plan to my clients so that they can have the money for living while they are saving for the future. Instead of dipping into your retirement savings for a new kitchen or bathroom, you use your investment savings such as money market accounts to help meet those needs. It is all part of sticking to your plan.

Talk to your financial advisor about your options and choices. Remember that you need to be disciplined once your plan is in place. If you need to make adjustments speak with your financial advisor. I know you hear that a lot, but the relationship with your financial advisor is essential to the success of your financial plan.

I think by now you can see how passionate I am about what I do. I firmly believe that you need to have someone like that as your financial advisor.

Conclusion

This is not an ideal world. In an ideal world I wouldn't need to write this book. Everyone would have the time, resources, and support they need to manage their own money. We would all be well informed and well prepared, and choices would be straightforward and simple.

Unfortunately, we don't live in an ideal world. Over and over I have seen too many people unprepared and underfunded for their retirements. Consequently, their lifestyles suffer and they pay a price. The comfort they anticipated and the lifestyle they hoped for eludes them.

It's sad and unfortunate. And it doesn't have to be that way.

The key is to control your assets, all of them – including your time, your money and your advisors.

I sincerely hope that this book underlines the importance of taking control of your assets and the advantages of doing so. The examples in the book are real. You may find some of them may be hard to believe, but they are true. They actually happened.

The most important "takeaway" from this book is the importance of sound asset management, because it is the foundation of your retirement plan. If you have it, you'll just have a better retirement.

A comfortable retirement lifestyle begins with clarifying, writing down, and understanding your family's needs, goals and strategies. When you take the time to sit down and figure out what they are and why they are important to you, you are way ahead of most people.

This knowledge will help you recognize, and avoid financial professionals who don't have your best interest at heart. When you know what's important, you have a better chance finding the people who can help you get it.

We have seen how inflation, longevity, taxes, and market volatility can destroy your retirement savings and take a toll on your lifestyle. We have also seen that Social Security and many corporate pension plans alone are not going to be enough to fund your retirement. We now know that we can't depend on our government or employers for our security. We can only depend on ourselves.

Working with the right financial advisor who knows and appreciates your goals, needs and strategies is the key to managing these risks and controlling your future.

Throughout this book, I have given you the tools to recognize and steer clear of the risks of bad strategies, bad products and bad advisors, so you can build a stable financial foundation for your retirement.

Follow my advice and setup your "six financial plans". When you do, you could place yourself in a much better position for your retirement. You will help improve your chances of achieving all the goals you set for you and your family.

Remember, you have to start somewhere. By following my advice you will establish a benchmark, a place from which you can set up all six plans. Even if you only follow part of my advice it is better than doing nothing at all.

Of course, no one can guarantee a perfect retirement, but that doesn't mean you have to leave it to chance. There is a lot you can do to help grow and protect your money. I believe I've shown you a few ideas here. But as I said earlier, people don't plan to fail they fail to plan.

You may have even found some of the book a little scary. But, there are some unpleasant truths such as illness and death that need to be discussed. I am sorry if I have frightened you, but it's better to be a little frightened now than shocked and broke later. I firmly believe we must discuss these issues openly in order to plan most effectively for the future.

The shadow of long-term care needs and costs is a real and present danger in America. Our large and aging Boomer population means that the issue of long-term care will not be going away anytime soon either. It will only become more important.

If you don't take the steps necessary to prepare for that reality, you are not only putting yourself at risk, but also putting undue stress and financial burdens on the people you love. Long-term care protection is a gift for you and your family. You need to consider it seriously. Today is not too soon.

I want everyone who reads this book to take control of his or her assets. My greatest satisfaction comes from helping people build solid financial foundations. I hope this book helps you.

So take this information and look seriously and critically at your own situation. Are you in control? Could you use a hand?

If this book makes sense to you, do yourself a favor and pick up the phone or get in the car and make contact with a good financial advisor.

Go over your financial situation with the first advisor and then try to get second or even third opinions from other advisors. Take advantage of free consultations. Remember getting good financial advice is like buying any product or service. You need to be an informed consumer.

If you're sure you have your retirement under control, please pass this book along to a friend or family member who isn't so fortunate. The more people who can be helped the better.

The ideas within these covers will help you have a more prosperous, healthy and happy retirement. I sincerely hope that it will happen for you and everyone who reads this book. Control your assets and prosper!

Appendix A

What is an Annuity?

Let's start with the basics. An annuity is a contract between you and an insurance company, under which you make a lump-sum payment or series of payments. In return, the insurer agrees to make periodic payments to you beginning immediately or at some future date.

Money in an annuity grows tax-deferred until an income is received. It may also include a death benefit that will pay your beneficiary a guaranteed minimum amount, such as your total purchase payments at a minimum (Based on the claims paying ability of the issuer).

The three Annuity Phases

When you consider purchasing annuities you should first consider them as a long-term investment. I like to look at annuities as having three phases.

The first is the **Accumulation phase**. This is the period when your annuity is building up your wealth. The length of time depends on how long you have to save before retirement. Typically the accumulation phase lasts at least ten years. However, you can have shorter periods as well.

Next comes the **Income phase**. This is when you withdraw money from your annuity to provide income for your retirement. Depending on the product you can withdraw a certain percentage of your savings to provide you with a source of income. The thing that I like about annuities is that they can provide a steady stream of income. Instead of taking all your money out once you retire, you can set up a fixed annual withdrawal amount based on your needs. That way you aren't taking out more money than you need, and most importantly, you are not paying more tax than you have to.

The last part is the **Wealth Transfer phase**. Annuities are unique in that they not only provide you with savings and income, but they also allow you to transfer your unused savings to loved ones in the form of death benefits.

Types of Annuities

There are several different kinds of annuities. Four of the most common are the following:

Single premium immediate annuity

With a single premium immediate annuity you pay the insurance company a lump sum now and begin to receive withdrawal distributions in approximately one month and for a period of time you specify. The amount you receive will vary according to the length of time the payments are to last and whether anyone will receive the remaining balance at your death. Your money grows at a fixed interest rate, set each year by the insurance company.

Single premium deferred annuity

With a single premium deferred annuity you pay the insurance company a lump sum now and defer receiving withdrawals until later. The amount of those distributions will depend on the value of your account at the time your payments begin, the length of time the payments are to last, and whether anyone will receive the remaining balance at your death. Your money grows at a fixed interest rate, set each year by the insurance company.

Annual premium deferred annuity

With an annual premium deferred annuity you send money to the insurance company usually monthly, quarterly, or annually. Your money earns a fixed interest rate, set each year by the insurance company, and you defer your withdrawals to a later date to provide an income.

Variable annuity

This annuity is a vehicle that allows you to take advantage of equity investments. You can do a one-time deposit or contribute throughout the life of the contract. You have choices as to how your money is invested, and you may invest conservatively or aggressively. The growth of your account value will vary, depending on your choice of investments.

While those four are the most common, I want to touch on equity-indexed annuities.

Equity-indexed annuity

Equity Indexed Annuities or EIAs are complex financial instruments that include features of both fixed and variable annuities. Their return varies more than a fixed annuity, but not as much as a variable annuity. So EIAs give you more risk (but more potential return) than a fixed annuity but less risk (and less potential return) than a variable annuity.

EIAs offer a minimum guaranteed interest rate combined with an interest rate linked to a market index. Because of the guaranteed interest rate, EIAs have less market risk than variable annuities. EIAs also have the potential to earn returns better than traditional fixed annuities when the stock market is rising.

It is important to remember that EIAs are long-term investments. Getting out early may mean taking a loss. Many EIAs have surrender charges.

The surrender charge can be a percentage of the amount withdrawn or a reduction in the interest rate credited to the EIA.

Also, any withdrawals from tax-deferred annuities before you reach the age of 59½ are generally subject to a 10 per cent tax penalty in addition to any gain being taxed as ordinary income.

Because of the complex nature of EIAs, it is important to get as much information as possible before purchasing. For a more detailed description of the benefits and risks of EIAs I suggest that you speak to a trusted advisor or refer to the FINRA website.

Appendix B

Traditional or Defined Pension Plans

A defined benefit pension plan, also known as a traditional plan, is the type of pension plan that your father or grandfather probably had. The employer puts money aside for you, manages it, and guarantees you a specific amount of money for life upon your retirement. The total amount of your pension depends on how long you have worked for the company and how much money you've earned over the years.

These types of plans usually begin paying your benefits when you reach retirement age and stop working. Benefits will continue for as long as you live. Most defined benefit plans pay you a monthly check. Some give you the option, instead, to receive one lump-sum payment when you retire.

In most defined benefit plans, you must participate for a certain number of years before you have a legal right to receive the benefits.

These types of plans are becoming very rare today, as they require significant capital on the part of the employer. A good example of how much of an impact traditional pension plans can have on a company is the automobile industry. I like to joke that General Motors and Ford are pension plans that happen to make cars. The truth is that if the largest automobile makers in the world can't survive because of the burden of pension commitments, how well would smaller companies fare? As a result, most companies have moved to the employer sponsored plans.

Employer Sponsored Plans

When talking about employer-sponsored plans, most of you are familiar with the 401K. But did you know that there are actually three types of employer-sponsored plans? These plans all function the same way, the primary difference is that they operate in different sectors. Here is how they work.

A 401K plan is a private-company sponsored qualified retirement plan for employees. A 457 plan is for public and non-profit companies, such as charitable foundations. And a 403 (b) plan is for educational and non-profit organizations such as schools.

Contributions and earnings in a 401K plan are not subject to federal and most state income taxes until the funds are withdrawn. A 401K plan allows you to save money on a pretax basis with most employers contributing matching funds to make the plan even more lucrative.

Individual Retirement Accounts

An Individual Retirement Account (IRA) is a plan that allows a person to make contributions each year if they meet the <u>contribution requirements</u>. If you are age 50 or older, you can contribute even more to your IRA.

Anyone can contribute to a traditional IRA if he/she has earned income for the year at least equal to the amount of the contribution and are under the age of 70.5. If a person has a company sponsored retirement plan, there might be limitations on how much can be contributed to a traditional IRA. Depending on income and filing status, there could be a <u>limitation</u> on how much can be deducted from taxes. There is no age limit for contributing to a Roth IRA provided the earned income condition is met. There are <u>phase-out rules</u> in place for how much a highly paid person can contribute to a Roth IRA.

A simple IRA is an employer sponsored plan where plan contributions are made to a participating employee's IRA. The tax-deferred contributions are higher than a traditional or Roth IRA.

Roth IRAs were created in 1997 to help middle-class Americans. These IRAs are not tax-deductible, but provide even greater flexibility than traditional IRAs. Contributions to the account can be withdrawn at any time without being subject to penalty or tax, though interest earned in the account is. After five years, both contributions and earnings in the account can be withdrawn without penalty or taxation. The same benefits concerning education and housing also apply as with the traditional IRA.

Any individual can establish and fund a Roth IRA in the year that they have taxable compensation or self-employment income.

Both a traditional IRA and a Roth IRA are individual savings plans to help you save for your retirement.

Choosing IRAs can be complicated, depending on your financial situation and you may require the services of a certified financial planner. Another important decision you may have is whether or not to rollover a traditional IRA into the new Roth IRA. Generally speaking, if the person is eligible, contributing to a Roth IRA is always more advantageous due to the fact that income taxes will not apply later when the money is taken out, provided the person adheres to all the guidelines. But be sure there is enough time to absorb the costs of the rollover, since it will be taxed as if you were taking the money out of the IRA

These differences can make a significant impact on your retirement savings.

Appendix C

Information and Resources

In Chapter 9, I mentioned the names of organizations where you can get financial planning information and check the background and credentials of your financial advisor. I have listed the contact information below to help you in your search.

These organizations are a great resource for financial information as well.

Financial Industry Regulatory Authority (FINRA)
1735 K Street
Washington DC, 20006
Phone: (301) 590-6500
www.finra.org

International Association of Registered Financial Consultants (IARFC)
The Financial Planning Building
P.O. Box 42506
Middletown, Ohio 45042-0506
Phone: 1-800-532-9060
www.iarfc.org

Partnership for Retirement Education and Planning (PREP)
National Association of Insurance and Financial Advisors
2901 Telestar Court
Falls Church, VA 22042-1205
Phone: 877-TO-NAIFA or 877-866-2432
www.PREPpartnership.com

The Society of Financial Service Professionals (FSP)
17 Campus Boulevard, Suite 201
Newtown Square, PA 19073-3230
Phone: 610-526-2500
www.financialpro.org

American Council of Life Insurers (ACLI)
101 Constitution Avenue, NW
Suite 700
Washington, DC 20001-2133
Phone: 877-674-4659
www.acli.com

Association of Health Insurance Advisors (AHIA),
2901 Telestar Court
Falls Church, VA 22042-1205
Phone: 703-770-8200
www.ahia.net

GAMA International
2901 Telestar Court, Suite 140
Falls Church, VA 22042-1205
Phone: 800-345-2687
www.gamaweb.com

Insurance Marketplace Standards Association (IMSA)
4550 Montgomery Avenue
Suite 700N
Bethesda, MD 20814
www.imsaethics.org

Life and Health Insurance Foundation for Education (LIFE)
1655 N. Fort Myer Drive
Suite 610
Arlington, VA 22209
888-LIFE-777
www.lifehappens.org

National Association of Independent Life Brokerage Agencies (NAILBA)
11325 Random Hills Road, Suite 110
Fairfax, VA 22030
Phone: (703) 383-3081
www.nailba.org

Women in Insurance and Financial Services (WIFS)
6748 Wauconda Drive,
Larkspur, CO 80118
Phone: 303-681-9777 or 866-264-WIFS (9437)
www.w-wifs.org